Frog's Day

written by Catherine James
illustrated by Aaron Cole

HARCOURT BRACE & COMPANY

Orlando Atlanta Austin Boston San Francisco Chicago Dallas New York
Toronto London

Frog rests in the mud.
"I'm going to sleep,"
says Frog.
And he does.

Frog jumps in the tub.
"I'm going to take a bath,"
says Frog.
And he does.

Frog sits on a rock.
"I'm going to listen to music,"
says Frog.
And he does.

Frog hops in the grass.
"I'm going to have a snack,"
says Frog.
And he does.

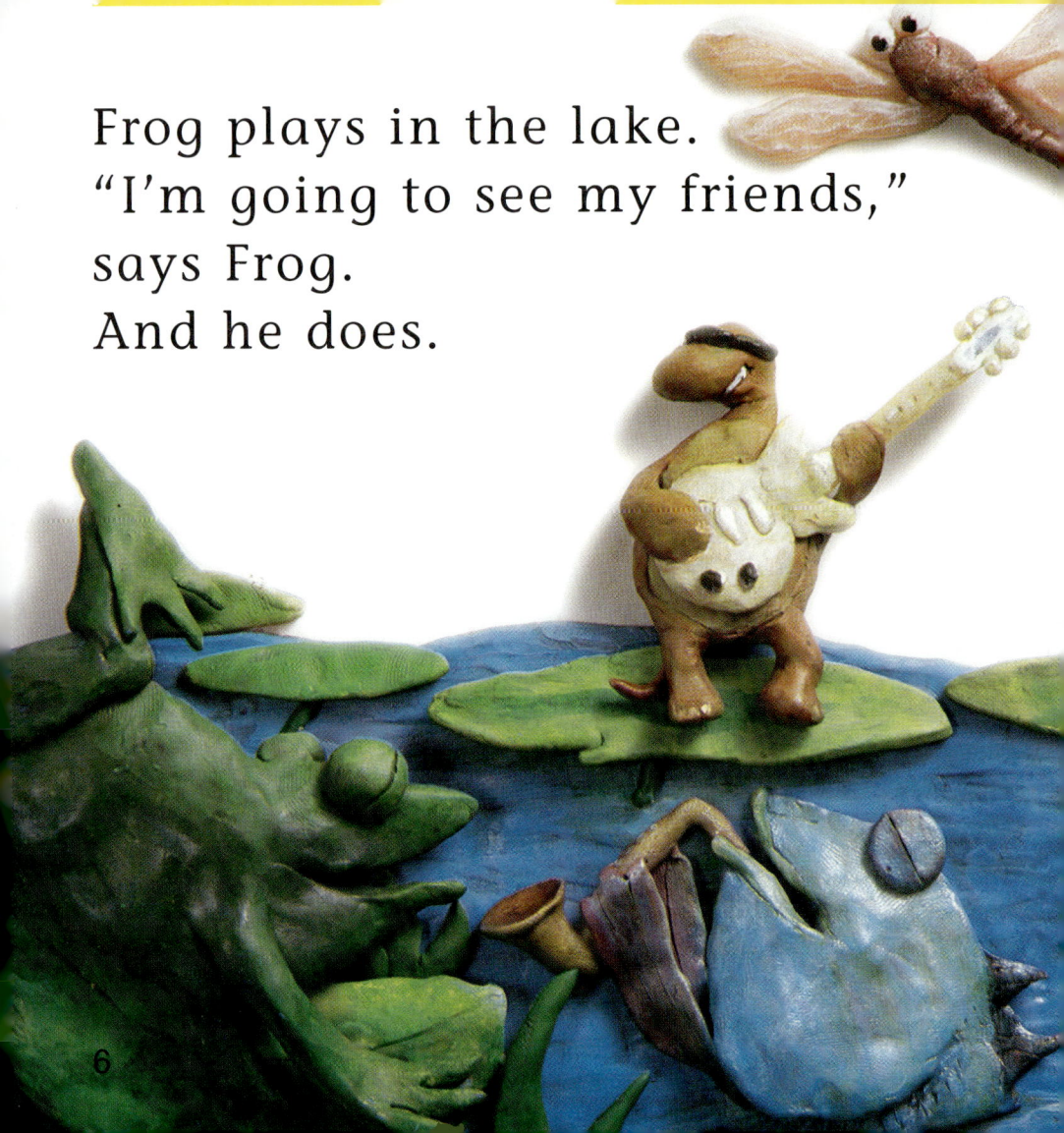

Frog plays in the lake.
"I'm going to see my friends,"
says Frog.
And he does.

What does Frog do now?

Frog plays in the band.
"I'm going to sing,"
says Frog.
And he does.
Oh yes, he does!